Fleurdelicious™

Written by Mary Beth Touzet and Renée Hemel

Illustrated by Amy Lee Story

AMP&RSAND, INC.

Chicago · New Orleans

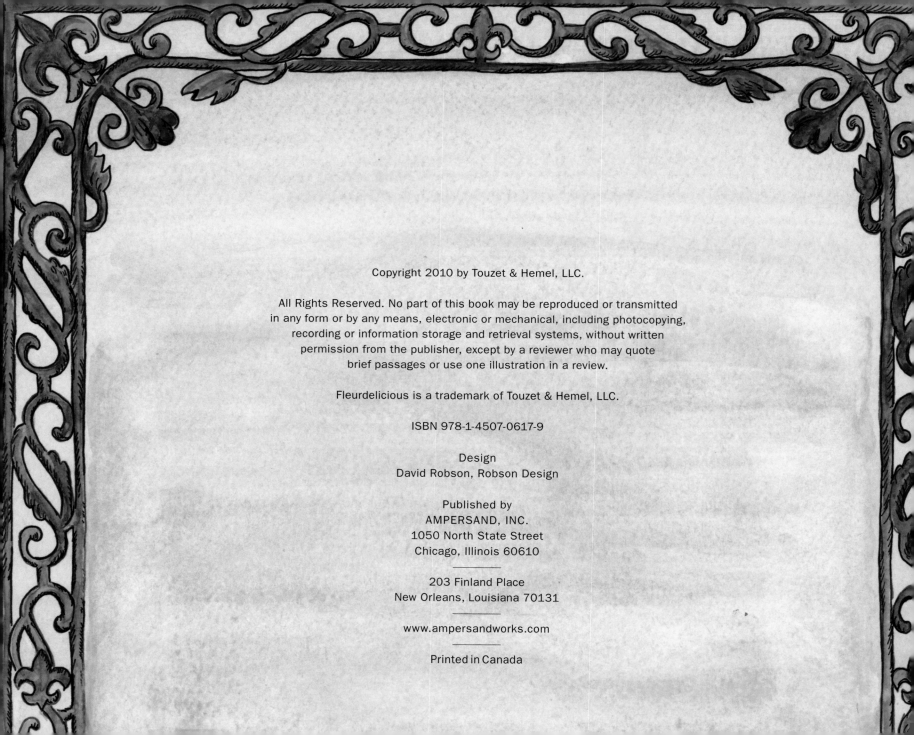

ISBN 978-1-4507-0617-9

Design
David Robson, Robson Design

Published by
AMPERSAND, INC.
1050 North State Street
Chicago, Illinois 60610

———

203 Finland Place
New Orleans, Louisiana 70131

———

www.ampersandworks.com

———

Printed in Canada

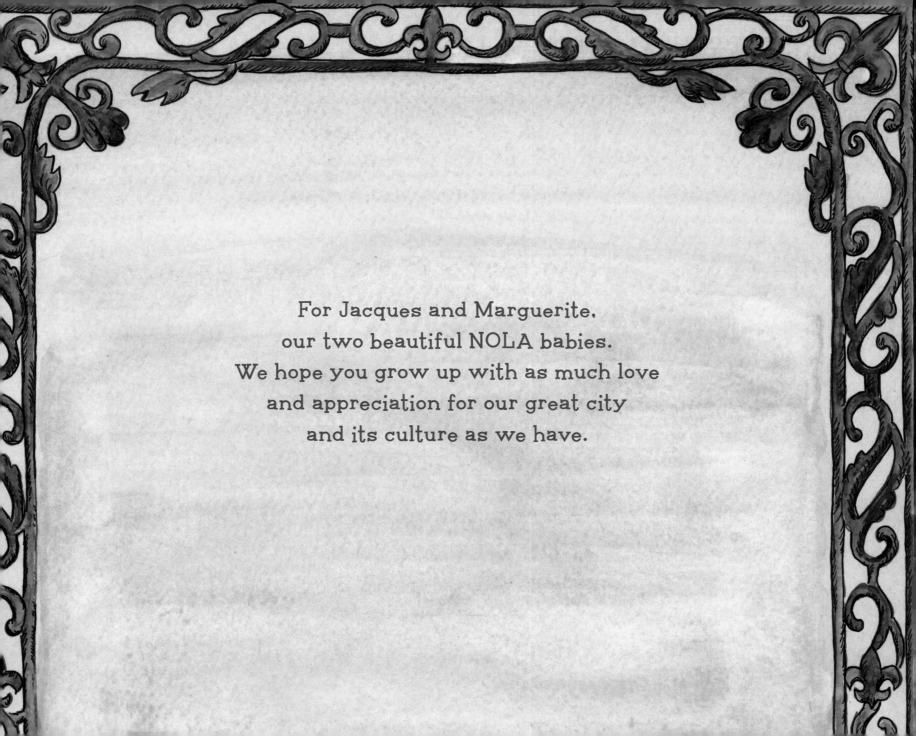

For Jacques and Marguerite,
our two beautiful NOLA babies.
We hope you grow up with as much love
and appreciation for our great city
and its culture as we have.

Fleurdelicious, a special fleur-de-lis,

Is seen all over the Crescent City.

From Bourbon Street to Esplanade,

And even Second Line parades!

She's on our flag flying high.
Even on dad's pink necktie.

She really loves going out to eat,
And French food is her favorite treat!

She's on iron fences and garden gates,
Even old buildings marked with a date.

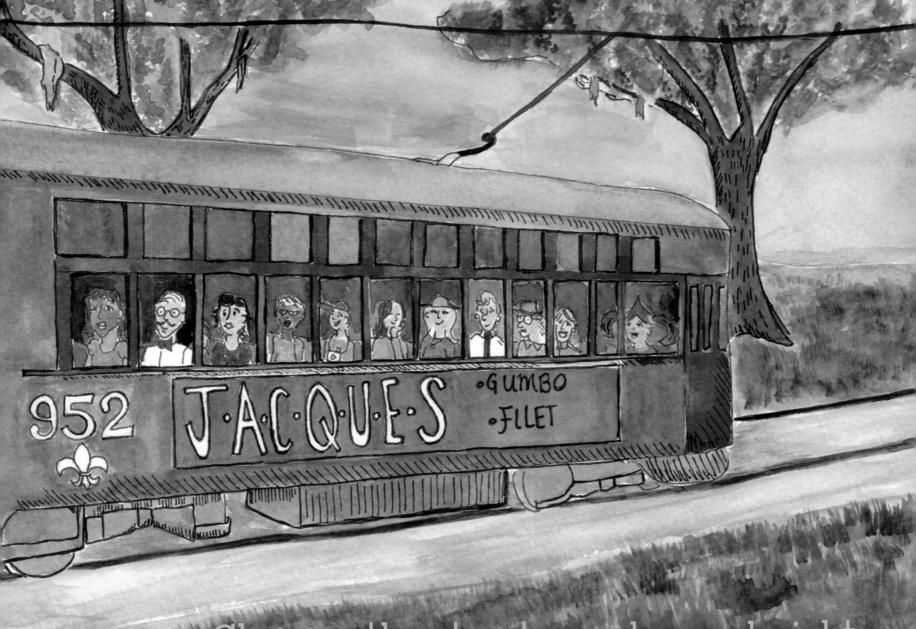

She's on the streetcars day and night.
Can you find her? Look to the right.

You might see her at the Audubon Zoo.

You know what they say: "They all ask for you!"

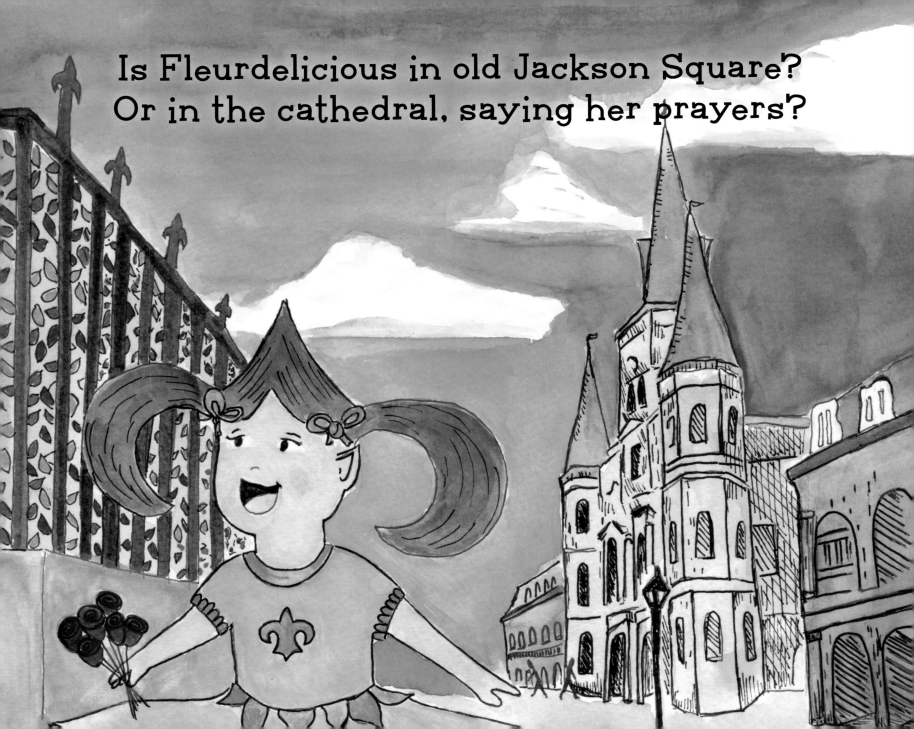

Now she's off to have beignets.
It's what she does on Sundays.

Is she riding the carousel in City Park?

Do you see her at the sno-ball stand?
She has EIGHT flavors! All made by hand!

Off she goes to a great Jazz Fest.

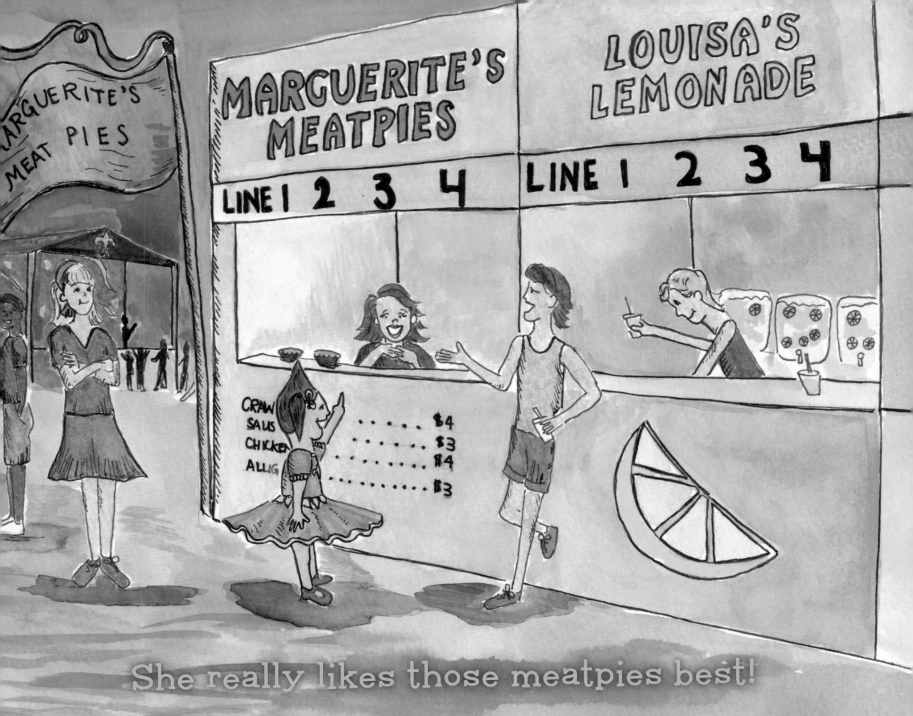

She really likes those meatpies best!

Fleurdelicious is here, Fleurdelicious is there! You can find Fleurdelicious almost anywhere!

WHERE WAS FLEURDELICIOUS?

1. **NEW ORLEANS CITY PARK**
   Where she rode the carousel

2. **FAIR GROUNDS RACE COURSE**
   Where she visited the New Orleans
   Jazz and Heritage Festival

3. **JACKSON SQUARE
   AND CAFE DU MONDE**
   Where she ate beignets

4. **LOUISIANA SUPERDOME**
   Where she cheered the Saints

5. **HANSEN'S SNO-BLIZ**
   Where she got a rainbow snow ball

6. **RESTAURANT PATOIS**
   Where she was served her favorite dish

7. **AUDUBON ZOO**
   Where she visited the animals

8. **CARROLLTON STATION**
   Where the streetcars sleep

About the Fleur-de-lis

Fleur-de-lis means "flower of the lily" and the symbol is a stylized iris flower. The fleur-de-lis has been found in the ruins of Babylon and other ancient civilizations. The early kings of France adopted this historic symbol as part of their royal emblem. It appeared on their shields and coats-of-arms, representing perfection, light and life. When the French claimed Louisiana and New Orleans, the fleur-de-lis was used to represent the monarchy. In 1918 New Orleans made it the official symbol of the city. In 2008 it became the official symbol for the state. Since Hurricane Katrina the fleur-de-lis has become an enduring sign of hope. Everywhere you turn, you'll see this beautiful symbol in our great city.